jE PARR Todd
The don't worry book /
Parr, Todd,

D0461742

To Erik

Also by Todd Parr

A complete list of Todd's books and more information can be found at toddparr.com.

About This Book

The illustrations for this book were created on a drawing tablet using an iMac, starting with bold black lines and dropping in color with Adobe Photoshop. This book was edited by Megan Tingley and Anna Prendella and designed by Jamie W. Yee. The production was supervised by Erika Schwartz, and the production editor was Marisa Finkelstein. The text was set in Todd Parr's signature font.

Copyright © 2019 by Todd Parr • Cover illustration copyright © 2019 by Todd Parr. Cover design by Jamie W. Yee. Cover copyright © 2019 by Hachette Book Group, Inc. • Hachette Book Group supports the right to free expression and the value of copyright. The purpose of copyright is to encourage writers and artists to produce the creative works that enrich our culture. • The scanning, uploading, and distribution of this book without permission is a theft of the author's intellectual property. If you would like permission to use material from the book (other than for review purposes), please contact permissions@hbgusa.com. Thank you for your support of the author's rights. • Little, Brown and Company • Hachette Book Group • 1290 Avenue of the Americas, New York, NY 10104 • Visit us at LBYR.com • First Edition: June 2019 • Little, Brown and Company is a division of Hachette Book Group, Inc. • The Little, Brown name and logo are trademarks of Hachette Book Group, Inc. • The publisher is not responsible for websites (or their content) that are not owned by the publisher • Library of Congress Cataloging-in-Publication Data • Names: Parr, Todd, author. • Title: The don't worry book / by Todd Parr. • Description: First edition. | New York : Little, Brown and Company, [2019] • Identifiers: LCCN 2018030944| ISBN 9780316506687 (hardcover) | ISBN 9780316556576 (ebook) | ISBN 9780316556606 (library edition ebook) • Subjects: LCSH: Worry in children—Juvenile literature. | Worry—Juvenile literature. • Classification: LCC BF723.W67 P37 2019 | DDC 155.4/1246—dc23 • LC record available at https://lccn.loc.gov/2018030944 • ISBNs: 978-0-316-50668-7 (hardcover), 978-0-316-55658-3 (ebook), 978-0-316-55659-0 (ebook), 978-0-316-55657-6 (ebook) • PRINTED IN CHINA • APS • 10 9 8 7 6 5 4 3 2 1

Sometimes you worry.

You might worry when you meet
someone for the first time.

When someone is being mean.

When it's dark.

When you are trying to sleep.

Or when you go to the bathroom.

When you go somewhere new.

When you are alone.

Or when you have too much to do.

You might worry when it rains.

When you get sick or have to
go to the doctor.

When watching TV.

You might worry when someone is being loud.

WOOF! BARK! AWOOOO WOOF! BARK!

When you go to school.

Or when you overhear some bad news.

Worrying can make you sad.

When you worry, try doing something to keep yourself busy, like talking to someone special.

Taking deep breaths.

Reading a book.

Dancing.

Exercising.

Or thinking about all the things
that make you strong.

And remembering everyone who

Worrying doesn't help you. If you are worried, talk to someone you love about it. It will make you feel better. The End. Love, Todd